MRS MOLE, I'M HOME!

BY JARVIS

WALKER BOOKS
AND SUBSIDIARIES
LONDON · BOSTON · SYDNEY · AUCKLAND

First published 2017 by Walker Books Ltd · 87 Vauxhall Walk, London SE11 5HJ) · © 2017 Jarvis · The right of Jarvis to be identified as author and illustrator of this work has been asserted by him in accordance with the Copyright, Designs and Patents Act 1988 · This book has been typeset in Butterfly Ball. Printed in China · All rights reserved. No part of this book may be reproduced, transmitted or stored in an information retrieval system in any form or by any means, graphic, electronic or mechanical, including photocopying, taping and recording, without prior written permission from the publisher. British Library Cataloguing in Publication Data: a catalogue record for this book is available from the British Library · ISBN 978-1-4063-6727-0 (hardback) ISBN 978-1-4063-7243-4 (paperback) · www.walker.co.uk · 10 9 8 7 6 5 4 3 2 1

MIX
Paper from responsible sources
FSC® C008047

FOR MRS JARVIS X

It had been a VERY long day
at work for Morris Mole.
Morris's feet were aching
and his eyes were
SO tired...

He couldn't wait to get home to Mrs Mole and the children.

But he had a problem!

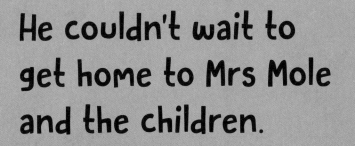

Morris couldn't find his glasses ...

ANYWHERE!

"Well," said Morris to himself. "I ought to know my way back home by now!"

And so, off he burrowed...

Up he popped!

"I'm not your wife!" said Mrs Bunny.

"You're not our daddy!" said the bunny children.

"Oh dear. Terribly sorry, my mistake," said Morris.

And off
he burrowed...

Up he popped!

"This isn't YOUR home," said the Owl family.

"You're kissing our tree!" said Baby Owl.

"Oh dear, bleugh! Yuck! I'm awfully sorry," spluttered Morris.

And off
he burrowed...

Up he popped!

"It's always cold – it's ANTARCTICA!"
said Baby Penguin.

"This certainly isn't YOUR home..."
said Daddy Penguin.

"Oh d-dear, g-good by-y-ye!"
chattered Morris.

SOUTH POLE

And off
he burrowed...

Up he popped!

"I'm home,
my darlings.
And – how marvellous! –
you've run me a bath!"
said Morris.

"This is our swamp, NOT a bath!" snapped Crocodile. "And you better skedaddle before we have you for dinner!"

"Oh dear, that's not very neighbourly!" yelped Morris.

NO DIVING

And off
he burrowed...

Morris had burrowed his way into many different homes...

BUNNY BURROW ~~(crossed out)~~

WHERE ARE HIS EARS?

GORDON RATZY'S

GO HOME, MORRIS!

OH NO, HE'S COMING!

OWL RESIDENCE ~~(crossed out)~~

WHAT A TWIT!

TWOO!

But not one was his.

"Oh dear, oh dear, oh dear.
I'll never find my way home!"
cried Morris.

But then he smelt something...
Sniff-sniff... Something familiar!
Something delicious!

Sniff

sniff

sniff...

WORM NOODLES!

Up he popped!

"Oh, I am SO happy
to see you!" said Morris.

"DAD! We're over HERE!"

"Oh dear, my mistake!
I can't see anything
without my glasses!"
said Morris.

"They're on your
head, silly!"
laughed the
children.

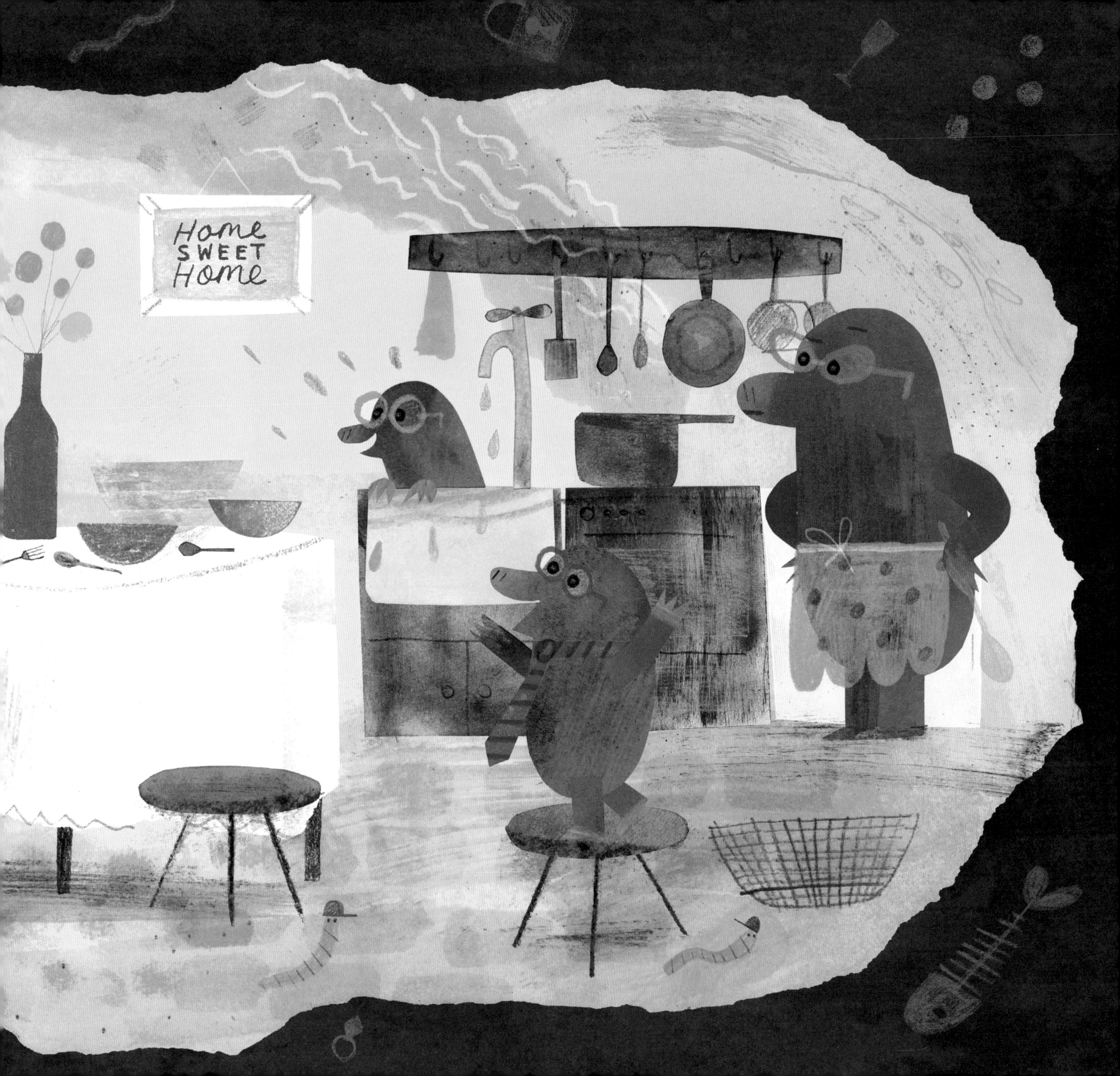
Home
SWEET
Home

"We missed you!
We were so worried!"
said Mrs Mole.

"And I missed you!"
said Morris.
"I will never
EVER lose
my glasses
again."

"Do you promise, Daddy?"

"I promise!" said Morris.

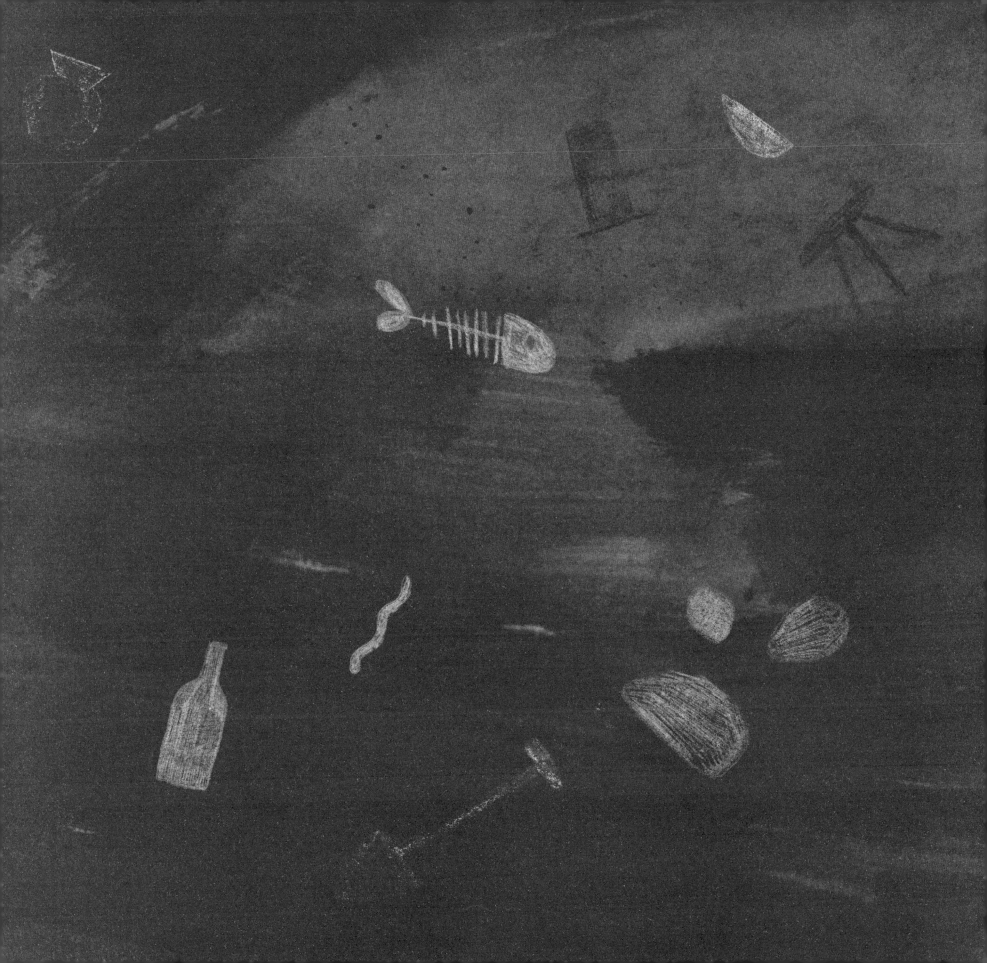

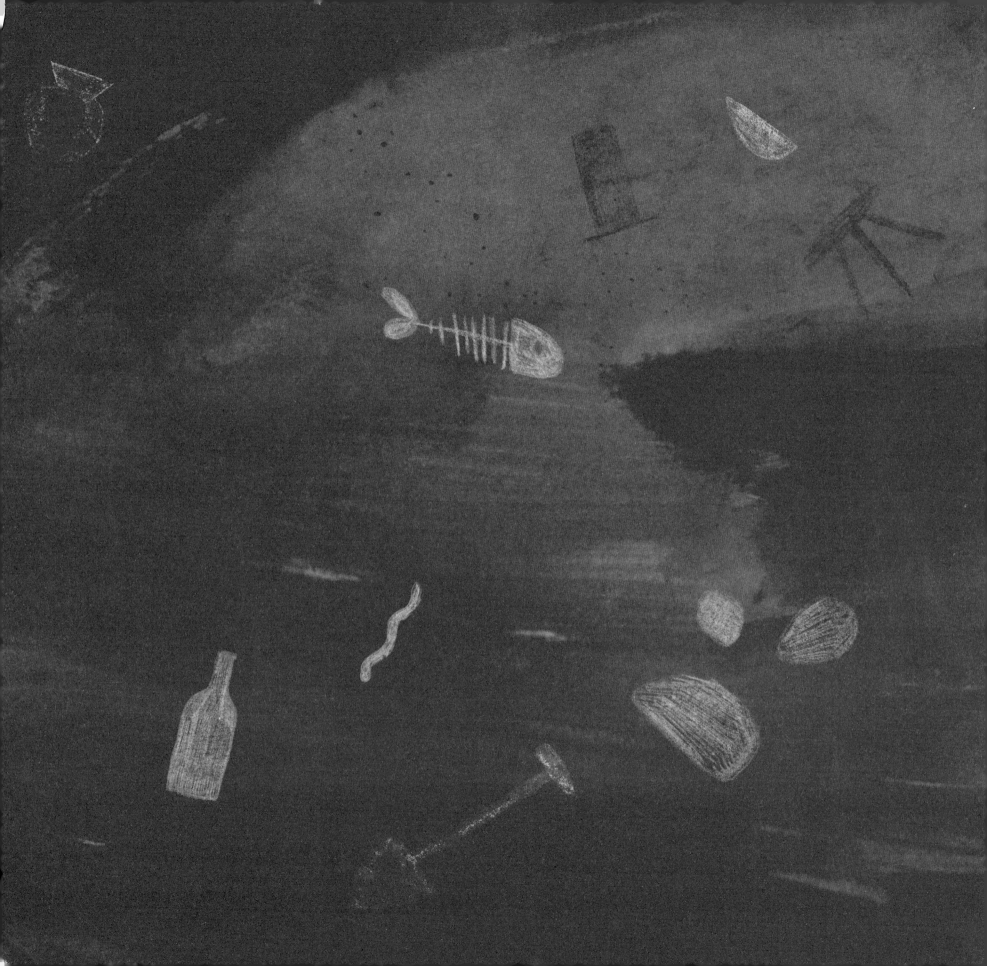